The Swallow and the Nightingale

Original stories by Oscar Wilde

Retold by Jonny Zucker

Series Advisor Professor Kimberley Reynolds

Illustrated by Qu Lan

OXFORD
UNIVERSITY PRESS

Letter from the Author

Growing up, I loved football and skateboarding and dreamed of becoming a professional athlete. There'd be victories, glory and even my own TV show! Sadly that wasn't to be, and when my skateboard snapped in half and I hung up my football boots, I

discovered reading. I found that books could take me anywhere – to shark-infested waters, distant galaxies and sometimes just round the corner.

One author I loved was Oscar Wilde. His short stories were clever and beautifully written, and two that featured birds really struck me. So when I got the chance to rework those very same stories I jumped for my laptop and got busy. Both stories are happy and sad – a bit like life really. I hope you enjoy them as much as I did when I first read them.

Jonny Zucker

The Happy Prince

On a tall column, high above the city, stood a statue of a little prince. His eyes were made of sapphires. His body was covered with gold leaves. A bright red ruby shone from the hilt of his sword.

'What a happy prince,' said the townspeople when they looked up at the statue.

One night, a little swallow flew over the city. 'I shall sleep between the feet of this golden prince,' he decided.

The swallow was about to go to sleep when a drop of water fell on his head.

How strange, thought the swallow. *There are no clouds in the sky, yet it is raining.*

Then another drop fell, but when the swallow looked up he saw that there was no rain. Instead, there were tears running down the statue's face.

'Why are you crying?' asked the swallow.

'When I was alive and I had a human heart,' said the prince, 'I lived in a palace. I played with my friends and I ran round the garden. It was a wonderful life and everyone called me the Happy Prince.'

'So what went wrong?' asked the swallow.

'When I died, my heart turned to lead and they put me up high here. Now, I can see all of the misery in this city and it makes me weep. For instance, there's a poor little boy who is lying ill in bed.'

'What boy?' asked the swallow.

6

'He lives in a street on the other side of town,' said the prince. 'Please, little swallow, will you take the ruby from my sword and give it to his mother? Then she can buy him clean water and medicine.'

'I will,' replied the swallow, 'but then I must fly off because it's so cold here.'

'Please stay with me just for one night,' said the prince.

'Fine,' sighed the swallow. 'I will be your messenger and I will stay for one night.'

So the swallow pecked out the ruby from the prince's sword and flew away, carrying it in his beak.

When the swallow reached the house, the boy was tossing and turning in bed.

The swallow dropped the ruby on a table and then flew round the bed, fanning his wings.

'This cool breeze is making me feel better,' said the boy, and he fell into a restful sleep.

When the swallow returned he said to the prince, 'Even though it is so cold I feel quite warm now.'

'That is because you have done a good deed,' replied the prince.

The next night the swallow went back to see his statue friend.

'Little swallow, will you do one more job and stay with me one more night?' asked the prince.

'What job is this?' asked the swallow.

'I see a young man trying to finish a play for a theatre director. He has no money for firewood and is too cold and hungry to write any more. Please can you take one of the sapphires from my eyes?'

The swallow agreed. Once again he flew over the city, this time with a sparkling sapphire in his beak.

When the swallow arrived, the young man was sitting at a table with his head in his hands. So he didn't see the swallow laying down the sapphire. When the young man looked up he was delighted. 'I will sell this sapphire for firewood and food. Then I can finish my play,' he beamed.

The following night the swallow flew back to the prince.

'Tonight I see a little girl selling matches,' said the prince. 'She has dropped them and they are wet through. She will get into trouble when she gets home, unless you give her my other sapphire.'

'But if I give her that you will be blind,' said the swallow.

'Please do it, swallow, and then stay with me for one more night.'

So the swallow dropped the sapphire into the match girl's hand and she skipped home, delighted.

On his return, the swallow said, 'Now you have no eyes, I will stay with you forever.'

In the morning, the prince asked the swallow to fly over the city and tell him about the poverty and suffering he saw. The swallow saw the rich in their beautiful houses and the poor with no food or warmth.

'My body is covered in fine gold,' said the prince. 'Take it off leaf by leaf and give it to those who are suffering.'

The swallow did this. But soon the snow came, and the swallow got colder and colder.

One day he kissed the Happy Prince and then fell down dead.

There was a cracking sound and the prince's leaden heart snapped in two.

15

The following morning,
the mayor of the town looked
up and saw the statue. 'How
shabby the Happy Prince
statue looks!' he cried. 'The
ruby and sapphires have gone
and he is no longer gold!'

So the mayor ordered his
workmen to melt the statue
down in a furnace.

'What a strange thing,' said
one of the men. 'All of the
statue has melted except for
its heart.'

He threw the heart onto a dust heap where the little swallow was also lying. Little did he know that this rubbish heap held the two most precious things in the city.

Even now, in paradise, the little bird sings forever and the prince is happy once again.

The Nightingale and the Rose

A young man was walking sadly round his garden. 'I know I should be studying but I can't stop thinking about my beloved,' he said. 'She told me she would dance with me at the prince's ball tomorrow night, but only if I brought her a red rose. There are no red roses in my garden, so what shall I do?'

A nightingale was listening to the man from a perch on the oak tree. *He must really love that girl,* thought the nightingale, *for his face is as pale as ivory and so full of sorrow.*

'I have no red rose to give, so I shall spend the night sad and alone,' groaned the man and he fell onto the grass, weeping.

Maybe I can help him, thought the
nightingale. She spread her wings and flew
down into the garden. At its centre stood a
beautiful rose tree.

'Give me a red rose,' said the nightingale
to the rose tree, 'and I will sing you my
sweetest song.'

'My roses are white,' said the tree,
'but go to my brother by the sundial and
perhaps he will give you what you want.'

So the nightingale flew to the rose tree
by the sundial.

'Give me a red rose,' said the nightingale,
'and I will sing you my sweetest song.'

'My roses are yellow,' said the tree, 'but go to my brother beneath the window and perhaps he will give you what you want.'

So the nightingale flew to the rose tree beneath the young man's window.

'Give me a red rose,' said the nightingale, 'and I will sing you my sweetest song.'

'My roses are red,' said the tree, 'but the winter has chilled my body and the storm has broken my branches. That means I will have no roses this year.'

'One red rose is all I want,' sighed the nightingale. 'Is there any way I could get one?'

'You must sing to me all night and press your heart against one of my thorns. Then your blood will flow into my veins and I will give you one red rose,' said the rose tree.

23

'But if I do that I will die,' said the nightingale. 'That is a big sacrifice to make for the sake of a single rose.'

'That is the only way,' replied the tree.

The nightingale thought carefully. The young man was so miserable she decided to get the rose for him.

When the nightingale returned to the young man, she saw he was still lying on the grass, crying.

'Be happy!' cried the nightingale. 'I will die to get you a red rose, but in return you must promise to love your beloved with all your heart.'

The man looked up from the grass at the chirruping of the nightingale but he did not understand what she was saying.

However, her friend the oak tree understood and he was sad. 'Sing me one last song, dear nightingale, for when you are gone I will be lonely.'

So the nightingale sang a beautiful song to the oak tree. The young man listened to the song and thought, *The nightingale sings beautifully but she only sings for herself. She would never do anything for anyone else.*

As the moon shone that night, the nightingale flew down to the red rose tree and started singing. As she sang she pressed a thorn against her body and her blood started flowing into the tree.

'Press the thorn closer,' said the tree, 'or the day will come before the rose is finished.'

The nightingale sang louder and pressed the thorn closer, and a flush of pink came to the leaves on the tree.

'Press it even closer,' said the tree, 'or the day will come before the rose is finished.'

So the nightingale sang even louder and pressed the thorn even closer, and eventually a marvellous crimson rose appeared on the tree.

'Look!' cried the tree. 'There is your rose.'

But the sweet-voiced nightingale had sung her last verse and she was now lying dead.

At noon the next day, the young man looked outside. 'What a wonderful piece of luck!' he cried, looking at the tree beneath his window. 'I see a perfect red rose.'

He leaned out of the window and plucked the rose. Then he raced to his beloved's house.

His love was sitting in the doorway with a dog at her feet.

'You said you would dance with me at the ball if I brought you a red rose,' panted the man, 'so here one is!'

'I am afraid it will not go with my dress,' frowned the girl. 'And besides, another young man has sent me jewels.'

'How ungrateful you are!' cried the man and he threw the red rose into the gutter. At once a coach wheel ran over it.

'What a silly thing love is,' said the young man as he walked away. 'It always makes you believe things that are not true! I think I shall give up on love and go back to studying.'

So he returned to his room, pulled out a great dusty book and began to read.